GW00493030

Puzzle
and
Colour

Compiled by Catherine Veitch
Illustrated by Chris Jevons

Miles
KELLY

Some Anchiornis like this are hiding on these pages. How many can you find?

All answers are at the back

Shade the shapes

Follow the key and use those colours to fill the shapes. Which scary dinosaur is revealed?

Key:

Which way?

Help this Protoceratops find its way through the maze to its baby. Watch out for the Allosaurus!

Q: How do you ask a dinosaur to lunch?
A: Tea Rex?

How to draw a Baryonyx

Follow these steps to draw your own Baryonyx on the opposite page.

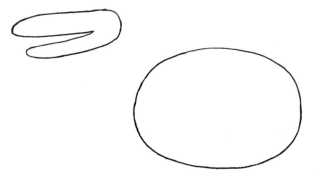

1 Start with the head and an oval body shape.

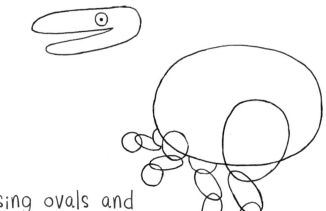

2 Using ovals and circles build up the leg joints, and add an eye.

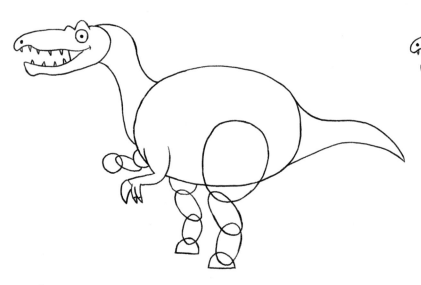

3 Join the head and body with a neck, and add a tail, teeth and some claws.

4 Finish the back legs, claws and add some texture. Raaaaah!

My brilliant Baryonyx picture

Now colour in your picture to bring it to life.

Q: What did the dinosaur use to mend its gate?
A: A dino-saw!

Puzzle it out

Which bit of Spinosaurus is missing from the picture?

1

2

3

4

Count and colour

This Oviraptor is missing some of her eggs.
Count all the eggs, then colour in the picture.

DID YOU KNOW?
Fossils reveal a lot about dinosaurs. But no one knows what colour dinosaurs really were.

Scramble and slide

Climb up the green Stegosaurus and slide down the blue Diplodocus in this fab dinosaur game.

1 Use coins, counters or mini-dinosaurs for each player and grab a dice or make a spinner for this game.

2 Take turns to roll the dice or spin the spinner and move your counter that number of spaces.

3 Scramble up the green Stegosaurus. Slide down the blue Diplodocus.

4 The first one to reach the end wins!

Can you spot and find these animals on the board?

Q: What do you get when a dinosaur blows its nose?
A: Out of the way!

Count the fossils

Look at all these fossils found on a dinosaur dig. How many bones can you count?

Q: What do you call a dinosaur that talks and talks and talks?

A: A Dinobore!

Odd one out

Look closely at this group of Velociraptor. Can you spot the odd one out?

DID YOU KNOW?

Velociraptor was a fast-running bipedal (on two legs) dinosaur. Its name means 'speedy thief'.

Spot the difference

Can you find eight differences between these two pictures? Circle them as you find them.

Q: Which dinosaur slept all day?
A: The Dino-snore!

Whose head?

These dinosaurs have lost their heads!
Draw lines to match up each head to its body.

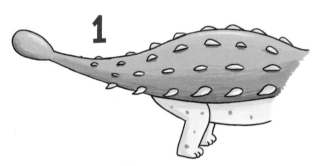

1

Ankylosaurus

2

Edmontonia

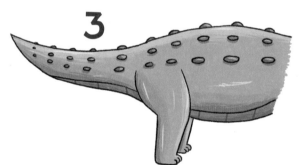

3

Scelidosaurus

DID YOU KNOW?

Ankylosaurus was covered in a tough body armour all over its body, except for its soft tummy.

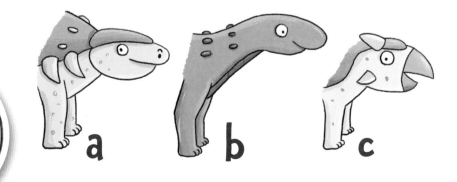

a   **b**   **c**

Dot-to-dot dino

Join the dots to see which dinosaur is hiding in the ferns. Use coloured pencils to finish the picture.

Q: What do you get if you cross a Triceratops with a kangaroo?
A: A Tricera-hops!

Answers

There are 5 Anchiornis altogether.

Shade the shapes
It's Tyrannosaurus rex.

Which way?

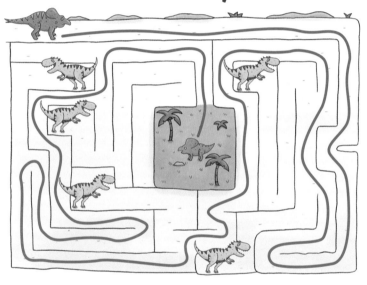

Puzzle it out
Number 1 is the missing piece.

Count and colour
The Oviraptor has 13 eggs.

Count the fossils
There are 11 dinosaur bones.

Odd one out
Number 8 is the odd one out.

Spot the difference

Whose head?
1c, 2a, 3b

Dot-to-dot dino
It's Triceratops.

Q: What do you call the dinosaur that lost his glasses?
A: Doyouthinkhesawus?